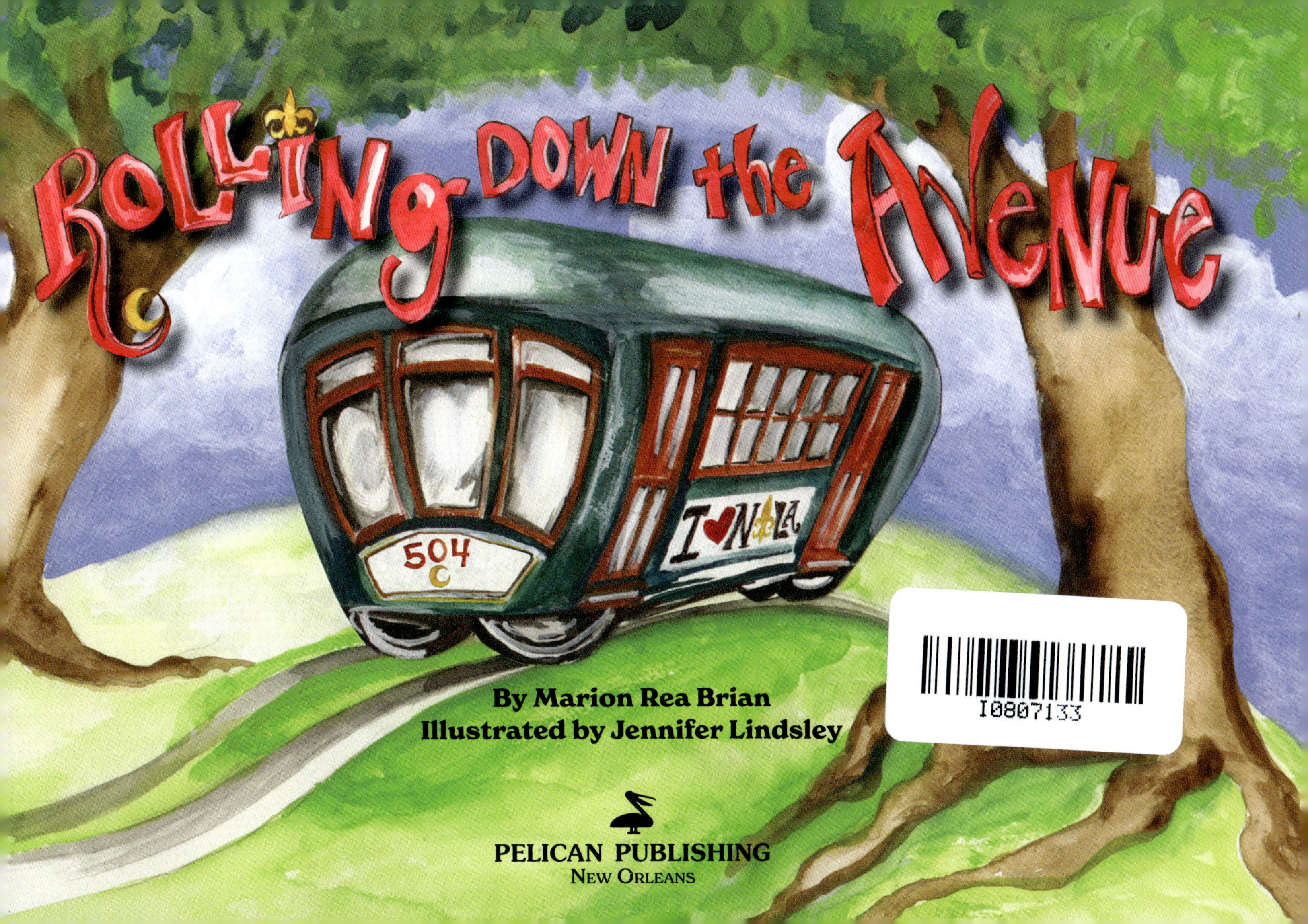

Rolling Down the Avenue

By Marion Rea Brian
Illustrated by Jennifer Lindsley

PELICAN PUBLISHING
NEW ORLEANS

First printing, 2016
Second printing, 2025

Names: Brian, Marion Rea, author. | Lindsley, Jennifer, illustrator.
Title: Rolling down the Avenue / by Marion Rea Brian; illustrated by Jennifer Lindsley.
Description: New Orleans, LA: Pelican Publishing, [2016] | Audience: Ages 3 and up.-
Identifiers: LCCN 2015032536| ISBN 9781455621798 (pbk.: alk. paper) | ISBN 9781455621804 (e-book)
Subjects: LCSH: Street-railroads—Juvenile literature. | New Orleans (La.)—Juvenile literature.
Classification: LCC TF148 .B717 2016 | DDC 917 .63/350464—dc23 LC record available at http://lccn.loc.gov/2015032536

Printed in China
Published by Pelican Publishing
New Orleans, LA
www.pelicanpub.com

For children of all ages who roll through New Orleans. Enjoy the view. May it bring you joy.

—M. R. B.

To my son, Haden, who colors my life brighter day by day.

—J. L.

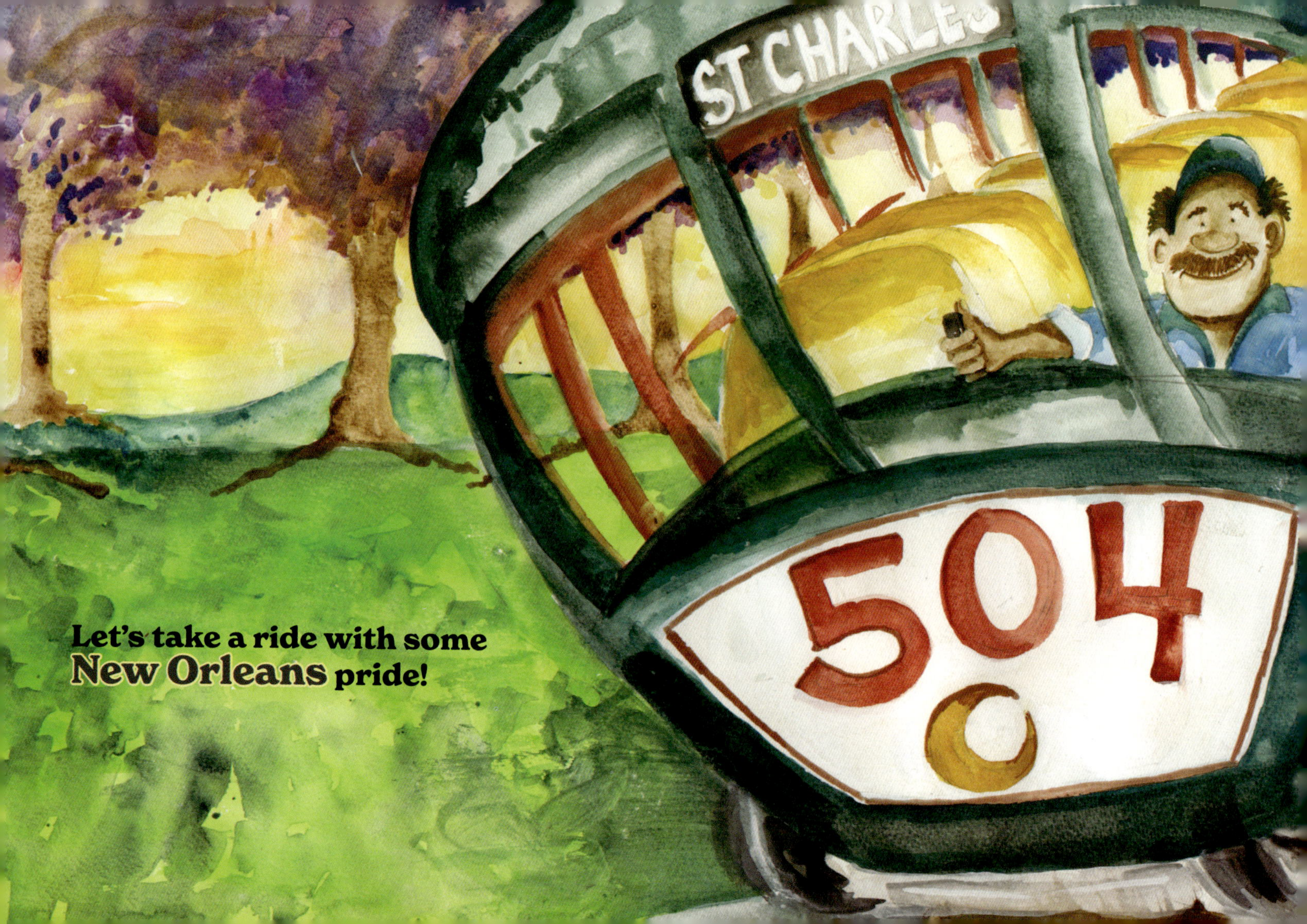

Let's take a ride with some New Orleans pride!

It will be **fun**.
On the tracks we'll glide.

Rocking past bikes, rolling past cars,
we'll even slide by other **streetcars**!

**Stand up. Hold on. Please don't fall.
We're hopping off now for a yummy
snoball.**

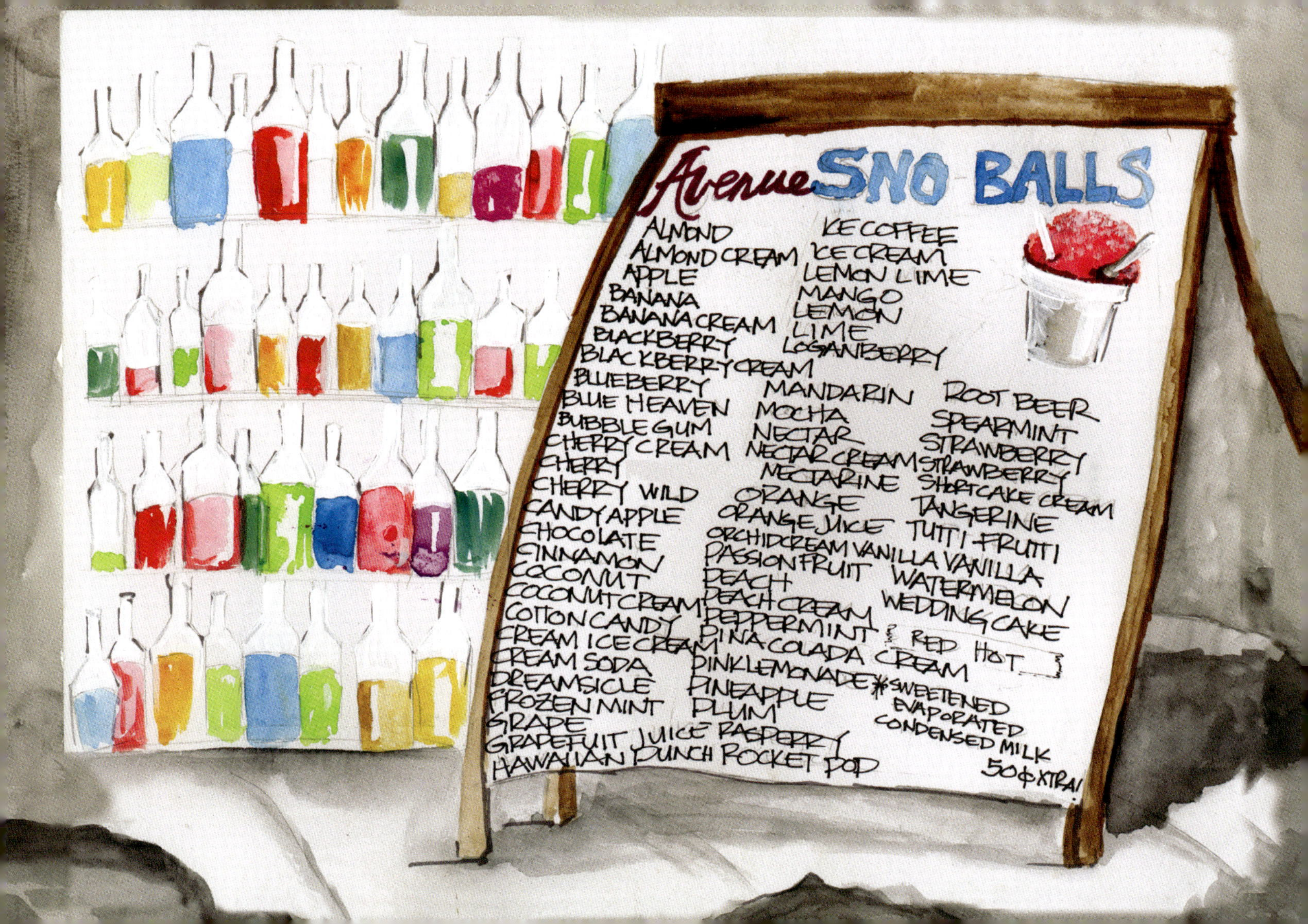
Avenue SNO BALLS
ALMOND
ALMOND CREAM
APPLE
BANANA
BANANA CREAM
BLACKBERRY
BLACKBERRY CREAM
BLUEBERRY
BLUE HEAVEN
BUBBLE GUM
CHERRY CREAM
CHERRY
CHERRY WILD
CANDY APPLE
CHOCOLATE
CINNAMON
COCONUT
COCONUT CREAM
COTTON CANDY
CREAM ICE CREAM
CREAM SODA
DREAMSICLE
FROZEN MINT
GRAPE
GRAPEFUIT JUICE
HAWAIIAN PUNCH
ICE COFFEE
ICE CREAM
LEMON LIME
MANGO
LEMON
LIME
LOGANBERRY
MANDARIN
MOCHA
NECTAR
NECTAR CREAM
NECTARINE
ORANGE
ORANGE JUICE
ORCHIDCREAM
PASSION FRUIT
PEACH
PEACH CREAM
PEPPERMINT
PINA COLADA
PINK LEMONADE
PINEAPPLE
PLUM
RASPBERRY
ROCKET POP
ROOT BEER
SPEARMINT
STRAWBERRY
STRAWBERRY SHORTCAKE CREAM
TANGERINE
TUTTI-FRUTTI
VANILLA
VANILLA
WATERMELON
WEDDING CAKE
RED HOT
CREAM
* SWEETENED EVAPORATED CONDENSED MILK 50¢ XTRA!

The CAMELLIA GR
ST CHARLES
504
I ♥ NOLA

Getting back on where the river bends,
we'll **wave** and **smile** to a few new friends.

Oh! It's the park!
What a beautiful **New Orleans** landmark!

I see colorful gardens, enormous trees,
turtles, butterflies, and even **bees**.

AUDUBON PARK

Leaving **Uptown**, still on the line,

There are
synagogues,
churches, and
homes so very fine.

Things that are old, things that are new
all blend together like **Louisiana** roux.

Under the interstate, over the tracks,
there's so much to see before we head back.

As we round the circle
and pause at the stops,
there are businesses, restaurants,
and many cool shops.

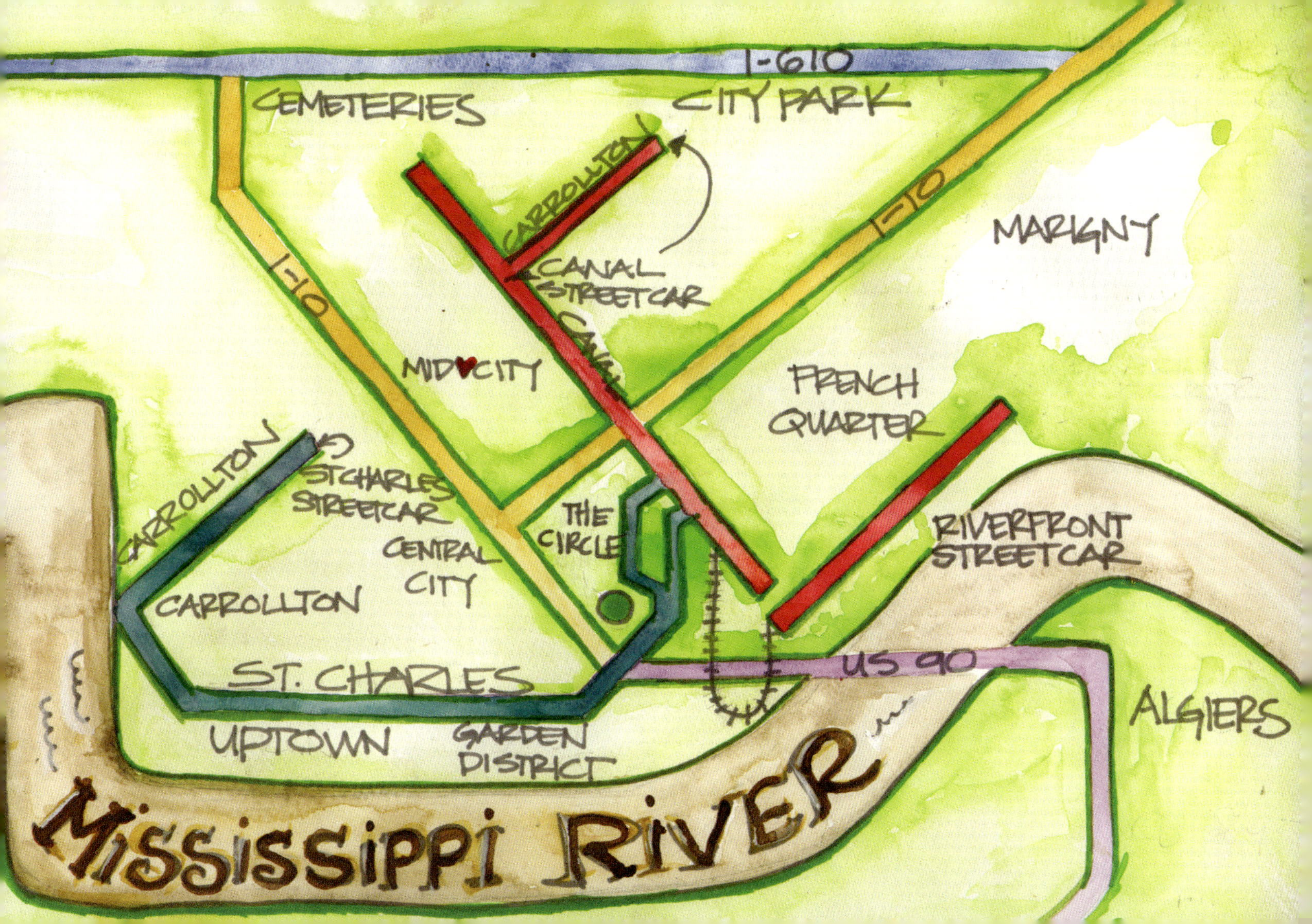

I-610
CEMETERIES
CITY PARK
CARROLLTON
MARIGNY
I-10
CANAL STREETCAR
CANAL
I-10
MID♥CITY
FRENCH QUARTER
CARROLLTON
ST CHARLES STREETCAR
THE CIRCLE
CENTRAL CITY
RIVERFRONT STREETCAR
CARROLLTON
ST. CHARLES
US 90
ALGIERS
UPTOWN
GARDEN DISTRICT
MISSISSIPPI RIVER

ESTABLISHED 1915
ROMAN CHEWING CANDY
75¢ A STICK

**Roman candy, muffulettas,
and po' boys too.**

**What an edible adventure
awaits me and you!**

Soon the green line ends where the
red line starts.
We'll get off here
to discover new parts.

The river is on one side,
the Quarter straight ahead,
Should we walk, take the ferry, or
board another streetcar instead?

A new ride leaves soon, with
destinations **galore**.
I don't want to miss it!
Let's hop on and **explore**.

Look from inside out.
Don't miss a thing.

Treme and **Mid-City** are
where beads in oaks swing.

So sit tight and listen close.
I know we'll hear some **jazz**.
Second lines and funerals
all cross these paths.

Restaurants, balconies, and cemeteries line the way.

Can you catch the aroma
of jambalaya and étouffée?

Our ride is over. What fun we had.
Rolling through **New Orleans**
sure made me glad!

The lesson from **New Orleans**,
when we reach the end, is . . .

Laissez les Bons Temps Rouler!
until we roll again!

AUTHOR'S NOTE

Riding a streetcar through New Orleans is a timeless treasure. I do it. My great-grandparents did it. I suspect my great-grandchildren will enjoy doing it also. Rolling along the neutral ground is a multigenerational, multisensory activity that is a unique Crescent City experience.

The green streetcars, which run along the St. Charles Avenue line, and the red streetcars that travel the Canal Street line have been rolling through New Orleans on the tracks since the mid-1800s.

At first, they were pulled by horses and mules. In the latter part of that century, the animals were replaced by overhead electrical wires, which are still used today.

Different, even newer red streetcars were built about one hundred years later, in the 1900s! These red streetcars run along the Riverfront, are a bit smaller, and have air-conditioning. They were almost all lost in the flooding after Hurricane Katrina. Each car was carefully restored and returned to the red line in the early 2000s.

From the 1800s, through the 1900s, and now in the 2000s, people have enjoyed the view. So look out the windows and enjoy it too!